Asla & Bergen,

We hope this inspires the
creative genius I witness everyday'
I LOVE YOU!

Nanny Allison

Sara picked this book out just for your FAMILY!

♡

# GIRLS WHO BUILD

Written by
Marisa L. Richards

Illustrated by
Folksnfables

Marisa L. Richards

Book designed by Folksnfables LLC.
(Team: Neethi Joseph, Athulya Arunprakash, Sherin Nazar, Indu Shaji.)

Content written by Marisa L. Richards
Sugar Grove, IL
https://www.mrichards.squarespace.com

ISBN: 978-1-66789-527-7

Library of Congress Control Number: 2023902930

Printed in the United States using FSC- and SFI-certified paper.

First Edition

For my girls, Adeline and Lucy.
May you always defy expectations, break glass ceilings,
and believe in your ability to change the world.

Construction work is hands-on fun!
Let's learn about the trades –
and the girls who get the job done.

# Adeline the Apprentice

Adeline goes to school to learn her trade.
Then she practices her skills on the job the next day!

# Lucy the Laborer

Lucy creates highways, bridges, and tunnels.
She builds up our cities and cleans up the rubble!

# Penny the Painter

Penny paints buildings, water towers, and homes.
She adds the finishing touch wherever she goes!

# Gracie the Glazier

Gracie installs glass windows and doors.
From aquariums to hospitals, her work really transforms!

# Ivy the Ironworker

Ivy builds bridges, stadiums, and towers.
She's part of a team – they can't do it without her!

# Ellie the Electrician

Ellie works with circuits and electrical wire.
She gives us energy, light, and power!

# Millie the Mason

Millie lays bricks and works with cement.
She's precise with her work and gives 100 percent!

# Etta the Elevator Constructor

Etta keeps our elevators moving up and down with ease.
She works in tight spaces and relies on her expertise!

# Olive the Operator

Olive drives heavy equipment, like bulldozers and cranes.
She jumps behind the wheel – even in rough terrain!

# Winnie the Welder

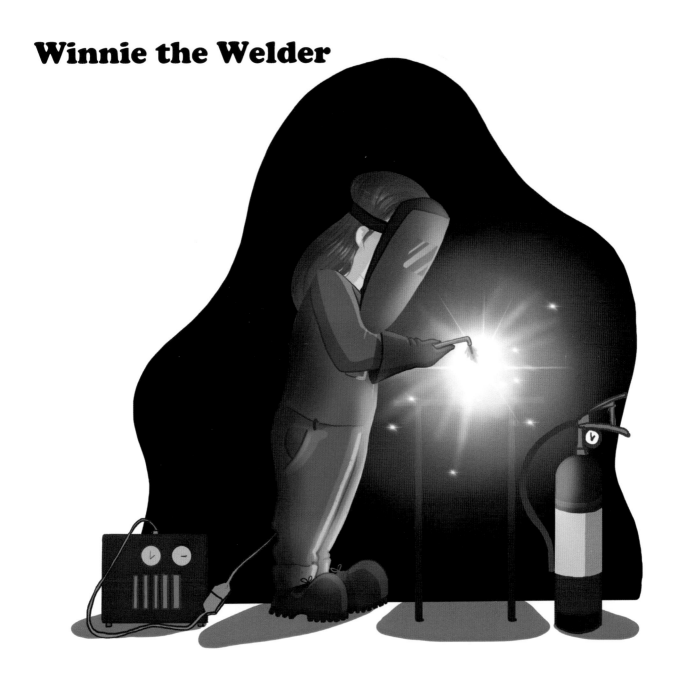

Winnie uses heat to cut and fuse metals.
From pipelines to airplanes, her work is essential!

# Ruthie the Roofer

Ruthie puts the rooftops on buildings at great heights.
She loves working outside and gives it all her might!

# Sophie the Sheetmetal Worker

Sophie bends metal sheets for air ducts and signs.
She uses math and design skills every time!

# Tilly the Teamster

Tilly drives trucks hauling lumber and freight.
She carries wide loads and she's never late!

# Charlie the Carpenter

Charlie frames buildings using wood and metal.
From basement to rooftop, she makes it all level!

# Dottie the Drywall Finisher

Dottie tapes drywall and smooths out the seams.
She brings blueprints to life with the help of her team!

# Polly the Plumber

Polly installs pipes that carry water, air, and waste.
She keeps our homes and hospitals healthy and safe!

Tradeswomen are strong, and fearless too!

These girls can do it, and so can you!

## ABOUT THE AUTHOR

Marisa Richards is a mother, wife, business leader, and IUPAT union member with over 10 years of experience in the industry. She currently serves as a program director for PDC 30, a union labor organization in Aurora, Illinois. Marisa studied writing and copy editing at the University of Illinois and received a bachelor's degree in creative writing and rhetoric with a minor in gender & women studies. She is an avid lover of books, grammar, learning, family, and female empowerment, and believes girls can do anything. Marisa enjoys drawing inspiration from her core interests and beliefs and is excited to begin her journey as a children's book author. She currently lives in Sugar Grove, Illinois with her husband Jake and their two young daughters.

## ABOUT THE ILLUSTRATOR

Folksnfables is a creative agency of illustrators and storytellers from around the world. We don't just tell stories about fairies and happily ever afters, we inform, educate, and entertain, in the hopes of nurturing a new generation of wonderful children, with values and themes that are important for the world today - like inclusion, diversity, cyber bullying, and caring for our planet. With radiant colors and child-like wonder, we create characters and stories that relate to you.

Folks who you'd love & Fables that inspire you.

Contact us at www.folksnfables.com
Instagram @folksnfables

# Eat Your Peas,
# Ivy Louise!

## written & illustrated by **LEO LANDRY**

Houghton Mifflin Company
Boston

www.houghtonmifflinbooks.com

The text of this book is set in Sassoon Sans.
The illustrations are watercolor & pencil on paper.

Library of Congress Cataloging-in-Publication Data
Landry, Leo.
Eat your peas, Ivy Louise / by Leo Landry.
p. cm.
Summary: Ivy Louise's parents encourage her to eat, unaware that the tiny green peas are
performing a circus on her tray.
ISBN 0-618-44886-1
[1. Peas—Fiction. 2. Food habits—Fiction. 3. Circus—Fiction.] I. Title.
PZ7.L2317357Eat 2005          [E]—dc22          2004009210

ISBN 13: 978-0618-44886-9

Printed in Singapore
TWP   10   9   8   7   6   5   4   3   2

for Ivy Louise

It was dinnertime.
"Eat your peas, Ivy Louise,"
said Mama.

"PEAS!" said Ivy Louise.
Ivy Louise rolled her peas around and around her tray.

"That's right," said Mama.
"Eat your peas."

## "PEAS!"
said Ivy Louise.

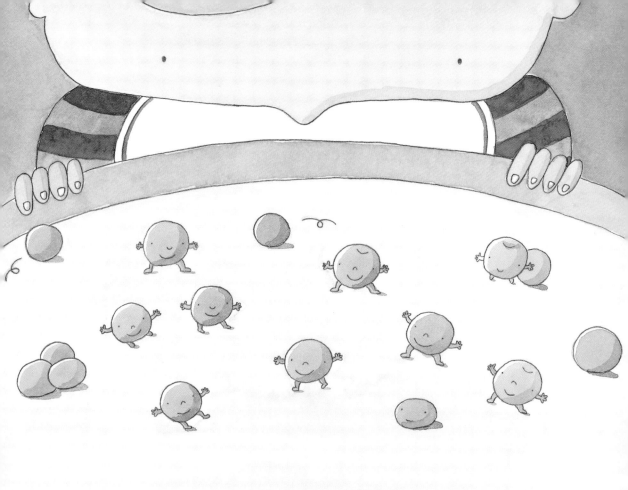

Ivy Louise watched the peas
roll around on her tray.

The peas quickly formed a pyramid.
One with a top hat rolled out to the center.

"Ladies and gentlemen…" he cried.
"Children of all ages…"

"Presenting the amazing, stupendous

Tender Tiny Peas!"

"**PEAS!**" said Ivy Louise.
"Good girl," said Papa. "Eat your peas."

And the Tender Tiny Peas
performed their best circus acts,
right on Ivy's tray.

The ringmaster continued.
"High above, may I direct your attention to Jumpin' Dave!"

SPLASH!

"Victor will now attempt to lift a mighty load..."

"Bravo!"

"Just marvel at those super-snappy,

roly-poly acrobats."

"Here come the clown peas...

Watch out, Ivy Louise!"

"And now, for our final act of daring and courage,"
said the ringmaster, "the Tender Tiny Peas
will make our exit, with your help, Ivy Louise."

The peas gathered together in Ivy's spoon.

"Now!"
yelled the ringmaster.

"PEAS!"
screamed Ivy Louise,
and...

# BAM!

She pounded her fist on the handle of the spoon.
The peas rocketed into the air,
perfectly aimed at the kitchen window.

"Goodbye, Ivy Louise," they called. "Goodbye!"

Out the window they flew,
landing in the warm summer grass.

Dinnertime was over.

"All gone!" said Ivy Louise.
"Good girl!" answered Mama and Papa.
"Tomorrow night, we'll have…"

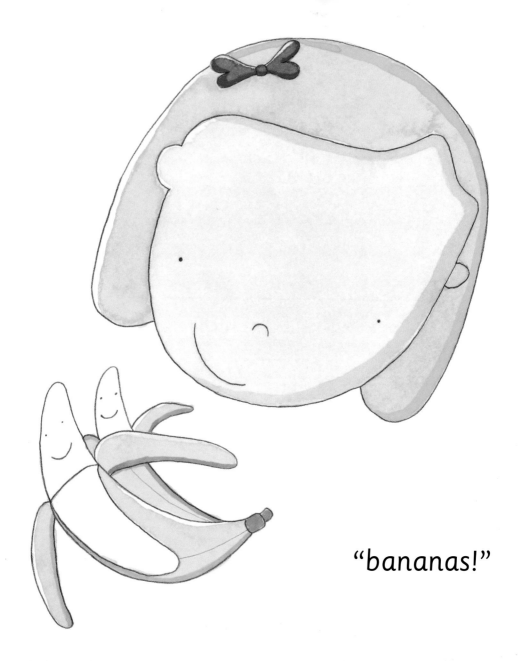

"bananas!"